Emily's

TIARA TROUBLE

SAMANTHA TURNBULL
ILLUSTRATED BY
SARAH DAVIS

ALLEN&UNWIN
SYDNEY·MELBOURNE·AUCKLAND·LONDON

Allen & Unwin
83 Alexander Street
Crows Nest NSW 2065
Australia
Phone: (61 2) 8425 0100
Email: info@allenandunwin.com
Web: www.allenandunwin.com

A Cataloguing-in-Publication entry is available from the
National Library of Australia
www.trove.nla.gov.au

ISBN 978 174331 984 0

Cover and text design by Vida & Luke Kelly
Set in 13pt Fairfield LT Std, Light
This book was printed in May 2015 at Griffin Press,
168 Cross Keys Road, Salisbury South SA 5106.

www.griffinpress.com.au

3 5 7 9 10 8 6 4

For Liberty, Jonah and
their awesome dad

CHAPTER ONE

Bella pokes out her tongue and makes a choking sound as if she is going to spew. I love that word. *Spew.* It's a disgusting word for a disgusting thing, and I usually want to do it when something disgusts me. Like now.

'What was that awful noise?' Bella's mum asks. 'Is someone ill?'

I erupt into a fit of snorty giggles.

'Emily Martin, what's so funny? This book isn't supposed to be amusing.'

Emily Martin – that's me. Bella Singh is one of my three best friends. The other two are

Grace Bennett and Chloe Karalis, who are giggling in sleeping bags on the floor beside us.

'Don't mind them, Mum,' Bella says. 'They're just laughing at me.'

We're all sleeping over at Bella's house. Our sleepovers are usually mega fun until bedtime rolls around. Then things become mega awkward.

You see, Bella's mum insists on reading us spew-worthy fairytales before we go to sleep.

Tonight, she's reading us yet another fairytale about yet another princess being rescued by yet another prince. And in *this* one, the princess just kissed a frog. Talk about disgusting.

'I just made that sound because I thought it was a little gross to put one's lips on an amphibian,' Bella says. 'I'm sorry. Keep reading, Mum.'

Bella's mum closes the book. 'Maybe that's enough for tonight,' she says. 'I'll let you girls chat for half an hour before lights out, okay?'

Bella blows her mum a kiss as she leaves the room.

'Thanks for having us, Dr Singh!' I call out.

Bella's mum calls back, 'Anytime, Emily.'

She doesn't get it, and we don't want to hurt her feelings. She and Bella's dad really do try hard to give the best of everything to Bella and her brother, Max. Unfortunately, their idea of 'the best' isn't the same as ours.

Bella's parents are the busiest types of doctors you can get. They're not the regular kind you make an appointment with when you've got tonsillitis. Her dad is a paediatrician – that's a doctor who specialises in treating kids.

Her mum is a neurosurgeon – that's someone who operates on people's brains. Most days they don't get home before nightfall and Bella and Max have to be looked after by their babysitter, Louis.

I have a hunch Bella's parents feel bad about being away from home so much, and so they try to make up for it with presents. They bring home every new toy, book or computer game as soon as it hits the shops.

The trouble is, they don't know what Bella likes. Max is easy to buy for because he likes all the things a typical eight-year-old boy is supposed to be interested in: bug catchers, Lego, comics and computer games starring superheroes.

But when it comes to Bella, her mum and dad don't understand. They buy her fairytale after fairytale after fairytale. Sometimes they throw in a doll. They even bought her a computer game once where you had to dress

up a bunch of animated runway models –
borrrrring!

Bella's mum and dad work such long hours,
I don't think they've taken enough time to get
to know her. Plus, Bella's mum was into
princesses and fashion when she was growing
up in India, so she probably just assumes her
daughter will like the same stuff.

If Bella's mum and dad really knew her,
they'd know she would much prefer Max's
comics – partly because she loves sketching
and partly because she's sick of fairytales.

I pick up the book Dr Singh left on Bella's
bedside table and start to flick through the
pages.

'What I don't understand is why boys almost
always get to be the heroes in fairytales,' I say.
'The princess, or the maiden or the damsel, is
almost always the one in trouble. And it's the
prince, or the knight or the king, who gets to
save the day.'

Bella takes the book and slides it under her bed.

'You're right, Emily,' she says. 'Fairytales should be called *unfair*ytales.'

Grace and Chloe laugh at Bella's clever joke.

'That's what you should tell your mum, Bella,' Grace says. '*Unfair*ytales are unfair to girls. She'd understand. She used to be a girl before she was a grown-up.'

Before Bella can speak, Dr Singh reappears armed with a parcel tied up in pink ribbon.

'I almost forgot about this,' she says. 'I bought you this fairytale today, Bella. Shall I read it to everyone now?'

Dr Singh looks eager to share the new book with us and I can tell Bella doesn't want to make her sad by saying no.

'Why not,' Bella says. 'It is brand new, after all.'

Her mum opens the book. 'Once upon a time there was a princess who lived in a big castle...'

Bella's too polite. If Dr Singh were my mum I would've told her a long time ago to ditch the spew-worthy fairytales.

But it's not my place to argue, so I zip my lips and count the stripes on Bella's bedroom wallpaper. Counting is one of my things – I'm a mathematician and computer expert. My favourite number is twenty-three because it's the only prime number that consists of two consecutive prime numbers.

As I count the fifty-seven stripes on Bella's wall, my mind drifts off while I imagine what my own castle would look like. It would have a drawbridge and a moat with crocodiles in it. Twenty-three crocodiles.

CHAPTER TWO

My mum is smart, but sometimes she does things I can only describe as plain silly.

My little sister Ava and I are watching her pull the hairs out of her eyebrows with a pair of pointy tweezers. She's pulling so many that I'm afraid she won't have any left.

'Doesn't that hurt, Mummy?' Ava asks. 'Your skin is turning red.'

Mum's reflection smiles at us from the mirror. 'Eyebrows frame the face. It's important to make them the right shape.'

I would've thought the right shape for

eyebrows was the one you were born with, but I know there are plenty of people who agree with Mum's theory. I've seen them lining up in our lounge room so she can pull the hairs out of their eyebrows too.

Mum is a beautician. There's a room next to the laundry that's set up for clients. She calls it 'the beauty room', but I call it 'the torture chamber'. It's full of freaky contraptions that cut cuticles, pop pimples and peel layers of skin off women's faces.

'Emily, do they look even?' she asks.

Mum wants my opinion from a mathematical perspective. If she plucks too many hairs from one side she can throw the symmetry of her face right off balance.

'The left one is longer than the right,' I say. 'If you take about two millimetres off the end, they'll be even.'

As Mum turns back to the mirror I can't help but blurt out what I really think.

'I still don't understand why you do it,' I say. 'It hurts, and it makes you look permanently surprised. You wouldn't catch Dad doing something so stupid.'

Ava's eyes widen, which tells me I may have gone too far. I shouldn't have said 'stupid'. I should've kept it at 'silly'.

'Well, your dad is lucky he's a man, because men don't have to make themselves pretty,' Mum says. 'It's just women who have to do things like this. I'm sorry you think it's stupid, because you and Ava will need to do it too one day.'

She swiftly turns and walks into her wardrobe in a huff. Ava runs after her, pushing past the dresses and stumbling over the shoes.

'Mummy, I like my eyebrows,' Ava says. 'I want to keep them.'

Mum bends down and runs her thumbs over Ava's tiny eyebrows. 'You're a long way off plucking, Ava – you're only five. Emily, on the other hand…'

I snort – it's what I do when I hear something ridiculous. 'Mum, I'm only ten. And I won't *ever* pluck my eyebrows. Not when I'm twelve. Not when I'm twenty. Not when I'm eighty. I think it's stupid... I mean, silly.'

'If your father were here, you would be grounded for that comment,' Mum says.

Dad is in the Army. He's overseas and won't be back for ages. Mum is right about how he would react if he heard me. He doesn't like anyone showing disrespect to his sweetheart, AKA Mum. But there's no way he would agree Ava and I need to change the way we look – not now, not ever.

I shake my head. There's no point arguing with Mum about beauty – it would be the same if she tried to tell me that algebra was a waste of time.

'Don't forget to take your ballet slippers today, Emily,' Mum says. 'You've got a class straight after school.'

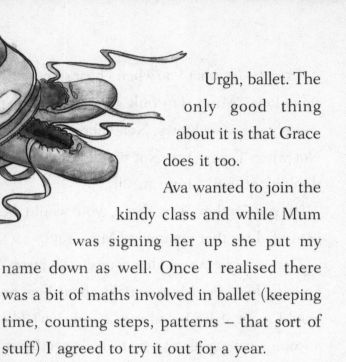

Urgh, ballet. The only good thing about it is that Grace does it too.

Ava wanted to join the kindy class and while Mum was signing her up she put my name down as well. Once I realised there was a bit of maths involved in ballet (keeping time, counting steps, patterns – that sort of stuff) I agreed to try it out for a year.

It's been six months and I'm totally over it.

'Can you let your ballet teacher know I just paid this coming term's fees?' Mum asks.

I guess I'll tell Mum I want to quit at the end of the term.

CHAPTER THREE

The blood is dripping out of Grace's knee like it's a leaky tap. *Drip, drip. Drip. Drip.* She says it doesn't hurt too much, but her white tights are getting covered in red droplets. *Drip, drip. Drip. Drip.*

'Someone's going to be in *big* trouble when they get home,' says Grace's older brother, Tom.

Her younger brothers, Oliver and Harry, chime in: 'Ooooooooh, Grace is going to be in *big, big* trouble.'

They run ahead of us, yelling, 'Trouble, trouble, *big, big* trouble,' over and over again.

We all caught the bus home to Grace's place together. The boys were at Scouts while we were at ballet.

Grace loathes ballet too, but her parents signed her up because for some weird reason they think all girls should love dancing. The only part we actually love is the end, because I get to hang out at Grace's house for an hour before Mum picks me up.

Grace could easily beat her brothers to the house, but she hangs back with me – I'm not a very fast runner.

Even though Grace is only ten, she is extremely fast. One of the fastest kids in town, as a matter of fact.

'Don't tell Mum!' Grace yells at her brothers. But we know it's useless. It's hard enough trying to figure out how we will explain Grace's bleeding knee and ruined tights to her parents. Having three obnoxious brothers dobbing her in beforehand makes it even harder.

Grace's mum rushes out to the porch, wiping her hands on a tea towel.

'For goodness sake, Grace, are you all right?' she asks. 'Come inside and let me clean up that knee.'

This is how it works. First Grace's mum worries if she's okay, then she starts to question her, and then Grace gets in trouble. If her dad is home the trouble is twice as bad, but it doesn't look like he's back from soccer practice just yet. He's a soccer coach – for boys.

'How did this happen, Grace?' her mum's questioning begins.

'I fell over at ballet.' It's a half-truth. Grace actually fell over *after* ballet. She was practising her sprinting at the bus stop and tripped over when one of the laces on her sneakers came undone. She didn't tie them properly because she was in too much of a rush to get out of her ballet jiffies.

'Why didn't Miss Charmaine phone me to pick you up?' Grace's mum asks.

Miss Charmaine is our ballet teacher. She knows we don't like ballet and she knows Grace didn't fall over in class.

'I…um…maybe she…' Grace can't think quickly enough.

Her mum bends down and dabs at the blood with a tissue. I can tell Grace's knee is stinging, but she's gritting her teeth and being brave.

Oliver steps in. 'She fell over while she was running at the bus stop.'

I roll my eyes. Brothers can be such dobbers.

'I was working on my sprinting,' Grace says. 'I have to train, you know.'

Grace wants to make it to the Olympics one day and I reckon she will. But first she wants to prove herself closer to home.

'We saw an exciting poster at the bus stop today, Mum,' Grace continues. 'It was for the Junior District Athletics Carnival. I've never been able to go in it before because I was too young, but this year I'll be old enough.'

The front door slams and Grace's brothers grin. '*BIG, big* trouble,' they all whisper.

Grace's dad marches up the hallway and straight to the kitchen. He's very tall with huge shoulders. Kind of scary-looking, really. He drops a bag of soccer balls onto the lino and stares straight at Grace's bleeding knee.

'Grace, how many times have I told you to

quit this nonsense?' his voice booms.

Grace's bottom lip quivers. 'But Dad, I need to train.'

They have this fight a lot. Grace tries to be tough but it always makes her upset. Her dad is so stern.

'We pay a lot of money for your ballet lessons,' he says. 'We can't keep replacing ruined tights, leotards and shoes. You need to learn to be a lady and stop running here, there and everywhere.'

He grabs a soccer ball and the boys follow him into the backyard. I listen to them laughing as Grace's mum finishes with her knee.

'That wasn't so bad, was it?' Mrs Bennett is talking about the scolding as well as the knee repair. 'Now help me with dinner, will you, girls?'

CHAPTER FOUR

INGREDIENTS:
1 small lemon
2 cups sugar
1/2 cup honey
1 cinnamon stick
6 whole cloves

'I'm sure I can make this baklava syrup better by having less lemon juice and making it up with orange juice instead,' Chloe says. 'I'd also like to add a vanilla bean.'

I'm not much of a cook, so I say, 'Whatever you think.'

Chloe takes three measuring cups from the cupboard. 'To support my hypothesis, I'll measure out three different flavour combinations,' she says. 'You and Yiayia can blind-taste and score the results against the original recipe, then I'll analyse the data and draw my conclusion. Sound good?'

I lick my lips. Taste-testing baklava is my kind of scientific research.

I'm used to being involved in Chloe's experiments. I see her the most out of my three best friends because she lives in the same street as me, in an apartment above the restaurant owned by her family. She lives with her mum and dad, her big brother, Alex, and her yiayia. *Yiayia* is the Greek word for 'grandmother'.

Alex gets paid to help out in the restaurant. Chloe would much rather have her weekends free to examine things under her microscope and hang with me, Bella and Grace.

Her mum and dad say that when Chloe and Alex grow up they will take over the business, but Chloe has other ideas. She is going to be a scientist.

Every now and then Chloe doesn't mind chipping in to help with the cooking if her parents are super busy. Her specialty is baklava, which is a sticky pastry filled with nuts. She says cooking can be fun when she's allowed to experiment. But that's the problem. Chloe's mum and dad don't like her experimenting.

'Our recipes are tried and true,' they say. 'Our customers know what to expect and that's why they keep coming back.'

Yiayia is more understanding. She knows that Chloe's favourite thing in the world is science and that changing recipes is similar to conducting scientific experiments.

'It's our little secret,' Yiayia says. 'We will pretend we don't taste the difference.'

If there's one thing Chloe loves as much as science, it's Yiayia. She's seventy-eight years old – that's sixty-eight years older than Chloe.

Yiayia is getting frail and she needs a lot of

help around the apartment, but we don't mind because she's wonderful company. She likes to read quirky facts out loud to Chloe and me from her old encyclopedias. We don't ruin her fun by telling her we can find all that stuff on the internet. She says reading keeps her mind active now that her body can't move so much.

Chloe finishes mixing the baklava syrups, complete with the new additions of orange juice and vanilla beans. 'Now, turn your backs while I pour the syrup into cups. Then you can perform the taste testing.'

She sets three cups in front of Yiayia and me. We taste the different mixtures and carefully consider each one.

'Definitely number two,' I say.

Yiayia gives a thumbs-up in agreement. 'The second batch is the best,' she says. 'Nice and sweet.'

Chloe makes some notes and tips out the first and third mixtures. Then she joins us in the lounge room and scans Yiayia's collection of dusty books. 'Yiayia, can you quiz us on the planets?' she asks. 'There's a science fair coming up at school and I'm thinking of making a diorama of the solar system.'

As she hands Yiayia an encyclopedia we hear the thunder of footsteps running upstairs.

Alex bolts in and kisses Yiayia excitedly. 'I have great news,' he says. 'I got the St Edmund's scholarship!'

Alex has been studying for a bunch of tests to get into boarding school. Not only do you have to be smart, you usually need a lot of money. A scholarship means he gets to go for free. This is big.

Yiayia rises to her feet and I grab her arm to keep her steady.

'Congratulations, *paidi mou*,' she says, pinching Alex's cheeks. 'I am so proud of you.'

Paidi mou means 'my child' – Yiayia says it to Chloe and me sometimes too.

Chloe mumbles, 'Congratulations,' and stares at the floor. Alex looks at her, waiting for a better response to his news.

'That's exciting, Alex,' I say to break the silence.

Alex nods in my direction. 'Thank you, Emily.'

He looks at Chloe once more. 'I thought you'd be excited, Chloe. Mum and Dad always said that if I got this scholarship you could take my place in the restaurant kitchen. You'll be earning some good pocket money.'

Chloe had been afraid of this moment ever since Alex started studying.

Someone would have to replace him in the restaurant on weekends, and it wouldn't be Yiayia.

CHAPTER FIVE

Every recess and lunch break, Bella, Grace, Chloe and I sit at the same picnic table in the playground.

Bella even carved our initials on the tabletop to mark our territory. I'm pretty sure our teacher, Ms Bayliss, has seen the graffiti, but she turned a blind eye.

Bella is one of Ms Bayliss's pets. It's not because Bella's a suck-up. It's because she loves class projects and always thinks of the most creative ways to present them.

Today Ms Bayliss brought in hundreds of

icypole sticks and some glue. She told us to make a cube, but Bella thought that was a little easy, so she made a skyscraper of cubes. It has nineteen floors and a rooftop deck. It would make a great hotel for ladybirds.

'Bella, what are you daydreaming about now?' I laugh as I open my backpack.

Bella's imagination gets carried away when she's dreaming of all the things she can sketch and build. She's staring straight through Grace, Chloe and me across the table. 'Oh, you know, I was just thinking of building a life-size hotel.'

Bella can be honest with us. Friends don't make fun of each other's big ideas.

Grace stands up, puts her heel on top of the table and bends over into a stretch.

'You know what else you could build?' she says. 'A stadium! Maybe I could make my Olympic debut inside!'

I wonder how many seats an Olympic stadium would need. Before I can start

to calculate, Chloe peels the lid from a container and a sweet, buttery smell wafts out.

'Anyone want to try some baklava?' she asks. 'It's my new secret recipe.'

We reach for the pastries. The sticky goodness makes us all groan.

'Mmmmmmm, Chloe, this is amazing,' I say. 'You really are a great cook.'

Chloe slumps onto the bench. 'Maybe that's my problem,' she sighs. 'Maybe if I wasn't such a good cook my parents wouldn't want me working in the restaurant and then I could keep my weekends for myself.'

'I thought your brother worked in the restaurant on weekends, Chloe,' Bella says.

'He's going to boarding school,' Chloe says. 'So I'm sure Mum and Dad will want me to take his place. I don't want to be a chef. I want to be a biologist or geologist or one of the other jobs ending in "ologist". It's SO unfair.'

Grace puts her arm around Chloe's shoulders.

'Well, I'd rather work in a restaurant than keep going to ballet,' she says. 'All I want to do is athletics but Mum and Dad say it's a waste of time. They don't think girls should take sport seriously. It's SO unfair.'

I frown. I'm getting angry. Bella, Grace and Chloe brace themselves. They're used to my outbursts.

'That's *it*!' I yell. 'Why do girls get one set of rules and boys another?'

I clench my fists and start stomping around the picnic table. If I were a cartoon character I would have steam shooting out of my ears right now. 'My mum says girls need to pull out their eyebrows and paint their faces to look pretty! No one cares what boys look like. It's SO unfair!'

The girls look perplexed.

Chloe speaks up. 'Did you say your mum thinks girls need to pull out their eyebrows?'

'Yes!' I screech.

My three friends burst into a fit of giggles. They have a tendency to do that. I join them when I realise they've never heard anything as absurd as removing a part of your face.

'We might only be ten, but sometimes I think we're a whole lot smarter than adults,' I say.

Bella's smile fades and I realise she has been a little quiet while listening to the rest of us whine about our parents.

'Bella, you're lucky you've got such a fantastic mum and dad,' I say. 'Grace's won't let her play sport, Chloe's want her to work in a restaurant and my mum is telling me to pull out my hair.'

We all giggle again. But Bella doesn't look so sure.

'I'm really sick of Mum and Dad treating me like a princess,' she says.

I know what Bella means, but some people think being treated like a princess is a good thing. Princesses live in amazing castles – Bella lives in an amazing mansion. Princesses

are showered in gifts from their subjects –
Bella is showered in gifts from her parents.
And princesses are really rich – Bella's family
is the richest I know.

'The princesses in those fairytales Mum
buys have the most boring lives,' Bella says.
'They're pampered and spoilt and sheltered
and no one knows anything about who they
really are. Mum and Dad try hard to pamper
and spoil me with toys and books and computer
games, but they don't really know me either. I
spend most of my time with the babysitter.'

I gulp. Bella's story could actually be the
saddest of all. Grace, Chloe and I might
complain about our parents, but we still love
them, and the thought of not seeing them
every day is very depressing.

I take Bella's hand. 'It's hard having my dad
away in the Army, but at least I've got my crazy
mum.'

Bella smiles. She's right that her parents

don't seem to know her. As one of her best friends, I can vouch for the fact she is not a fairytale sort of girl. None of us are. Bella loves to paint and draw and sculpt and build things.

'I don't want to be a brat and complain about the things they give me,' Bella says. 'But if they had more time with me, they'd get to know I don't want to be a boring old fairytale princess. What do any of them even do, other than look pretty and get rescued by princes?'

Bella has a funny way of putting it, but being treated like a princess isn't a good thing if you really think about it. Princesses aren't designers like Bella, athletes like Grace, scientists like Chloe or mathematicians like me.

The bell rings and we grab our bags.

'I just don't like princesses,' says Bella. 'I'm an *anti*-princess.'

We all link arms and head back to class.

I think we're all anti-princesses.

CHAPTER SIX

Chloe's biting her fingernails. She doesn't want school to end today. Every tick towards three o'clock brings her closer to the big question from her mum and dad.

'They still haven't officially asked me to take Alex's place on the weekends,' she says. 'They were too busy celebrating his scholarship last night to bring it up.'

We look at the clock. *Tick, tick. Tick. Tick.*

'Is it okay if I come over to your place?' I ask. 'Mum doesn't mind.'

Chloe nods. Yiayia loves it when Chloe's friends come over. She says the energy in the room is infectious.

The bell rings and everyone sweeps their books and pencil cases into their bags.

I start the short walk with Chloe back to her place.

'Why do you want to come over?' she asks.

'Mum's got lots of clients this afternoon so I don't want to go home for a while,' I say. 'Lots of crazy old ladies with layers of goop on their faces. They always want to pinch me and tell me how pretty I am.'

I guess I *am* pretty. I have long red hair, big green eyes and freckles across my nose. We are all pretty in different ways. Grace has short blonde hair, sparkly blue eyes and long arms and legs. Bella has brown skin, curly dark hair and braces on her teeth. Chloe has wavy black hair, olive skin and funky glasses.

But we're not obsessed with trying to look good. I can think of better ways to spend my time than sitting in front of a hairdresser's mirror or traipsing around shopping centres searching for new outfits that will be out of fashion in the blink of an eye.

Chloe and I arrive at the restaurant and walk upstairs to her apartment. Yiayia is in the kitchen brewing tea.

'Welcome home, *paidi mou*,' Yiayia says to Chloe. 'Your mama and baba are out buying supplies.'

I can see the relief on Chloe's face. She's escaped the kitchen proposition for now.

'Emily!' Yiayia opens her arms for a hug. 'How lovely it is to see you.'

I squeeze her tight.

We take a seat and Yiayia brings us chamomile tea. 'Tell me what is happening in your worlds, my girls,' she says.

We look sideways at each other. Where do we start?

'We're having problems with our parents,' I say. 'All of us – Bella, Grace, me and Chloe.'

Yiayia raises an eyebrow at Chloe. 'What are your problems? I won't tell your mama and baba if it's a secret.'

Chloe takes a sip of tea and sighs. 'Alex says Mum and Dad want me to replace him in the restaurant kitchen. And you know I don't want to do that. I'd rather spend my weekends behind a microscope than a sink.'

Yiayia shakes her head dismissively.

'Nothing is set in stone, *paidi mou*,' she says. 'Wait and see what they say. And anyway, you might be able to use the money you make washing dishes to buy that new microscope – it is expensive, no?'

Chloe shrugs. Even the thought of earning cash to buy science stuff doesn't make her want to work in the restaurant.

Yiayia stares into the distance. She has the faraway look in her eyes that she often gets when she's thinking about the olden days. 'My dear girls, how lucky you are to have such good friends,' she says. 'I remember when I was your age I had a group of friends just like all of you. We shared all sorts of secrets. We probably had a lot more problems, mind you, because our parents were a lot more old-fashioned.'

I find it hard to believe that Yiayia's parents could be more old-fashioned than ours.

Yiayia takes a black-and-white photograph off the mantelpiece. It's of a girl with wavy black hair like Chloe's. She's wearing a long white dress, frilly socks and sandals. And she has a huge frown on her face.

'This is me,' Yiayia says. 'Do you know, girls weren't even encouraged to finish school in those days? The only things we were taught properly were sewing, cooking and cleaning. Our shoes always had to be polished and we only wore dresses. And there were so many rules... we weren't allowed to giggle, or raise our voices, or run in public.'

Chloe and I drop our jaws in shock.

'You weren't allowed to *giggle*?' asks Chloe incredulously.

Yiayia shakes her head. 'Oh, it was very unfair,' she says. '*Tromeros!*'

Tromeros means 'terrible' in Greek – I've heard Yiayia say it before.

Yiayia's expression becomes mischievous.

Her voice drops to a whisper. 'That's why my friends and I started our own secret girls' club,' she says. 'We met every week in my parents' shed. It was a place we could be ourselves and solve problems together. No adults were allowed and the boys weren't interested.'

This is the first time Chloe or I have heard Yiayia mention any club. She must have been saving the story for a special moment like this. It sounds like an incredible idea.

I turn at once to face Chloe, and I can tell we're thinking exactly the same thing.

CHAPTER SEVEN

I run home from Chloe's as quick as my feet will carry me. I'm not as fast as Grace, of course, but it takes me about two minutes to run four hundred metres. That's roughly three-point-three metres per second. My brain just won't stop doing sums.

I fling the front door open and head for my room. Before I get halfway down the hall a thin, orange-skinned woman with stiff super-blonde hair steps out of the torture chamber.

'Excuse me,' I say as I try to pass.

The woman grabs my shoulders and leans

down into my face. She's so close that I can smell her perfume. It reminds me of toilet cleaner.

'My oh my, Emily, I could just eat you up,' she says.

Part of me is scared that she *could* actually eat me up. She looks hungry, and I can see her shoulder bones poking up through the skin. I want to suggest she try a hamburger, but I bite my tongue.

'My name is Fiona,' she says. 'We're going to become very good friends over the next few weeks.'

I have no idea what Fiona is talking about, but I can hear her tummy rumbling. I decide I'll call her Hungry in my head. I force a pretend smile and try again to make my way past her spindly outstretched arms.

'Emily, is that you?' Mum calls. 'Have you met Fiona?'

This is why I went to Chloe's place straight after school. Meeting Mum's clients gets in the way of valuable computer time.

Mum walks out of the beauty room with a weird metal contraption in her hand. I think it's for curling eyelashes.

'You were right, Lesley,' Hungry tells her. 'Emily's hair is gorgeous. It will really stand out under the stage lights.'

Stage lights? What is she talking about? I look at Lesley, AKA Mum, suspiciously.

'Emily, we've got a surprise for you,' Mum says.

She leads us to the living room and we all sit on the couch – me, Mum and Hungry.

Hungry gestures towards the coffee table. I see a brochure on it. I don't pick it up, so Mum grabs it and waves it in my face wildly. It's too close for my eyes to focus properly.

'You're going to be a star,' Hungry says. 'You're a knockout, Emily. I'm sure you'll win. I've never had a girl as pretty as you in any of my events.'

Win? Win what? I snatch the brochure from Mum and begin to feel dizzy as I read.

Junior Beauty Pageant

Are you a beautiful girl aged between 5 and 12?
Pull on your best dress and meet us at
the Lilac School of Arts at 9am,
April 6 for your chance to be a STAR!

I'm lost for words. Mum and Hungry look at me expectantly.

'Fiona is organising the beauty pageant that's coming to town,' Mum says. 'Ava's going in it too.'

My head spins. All I can manage to do is throw the brochure on the floor and run from the room.

'Emily, where are you going?' Mum calls.

I count the steps as I run upstairs. *One, two, three...thirteen, fourteen, fifteen.* The numbers help to keep my blood from boiling.

I burst into my room, slam the door behind me and hit the power button on my computer.

The email I'm about to type is now more important than ever.

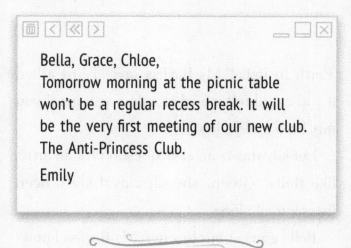

Bella, Grace, Chloe,
Tomorrow morning at the picnic table won't be a regular recess break. It will be the very first meeting of our new club. The Anti-Princess Club.

Emily

CHAPTER EIGHT

'Earth to Bella!' Ms Bayliss says. 'I just asked if you could tell me what colour you get if you mix blue and yellow.'

Luckily this is an easy question for an artist like Bella. 'Green,' she says, as if she'd been listening all along.

Bella grins at our teacher. Ms Bayliss knows she likes to daydream. But today Bella's doing more than just daydreaming. She's thinking about our new club – we all are. I just want recess to hurry up and come, but the morning seems to be the slowest in history (I know that's not mathematically possible, by the way).

Class finally finishes and we dash to the picnic table with Grace and Chloe.

Everyone sits and stares at me, waiting for me to speak first. I was the one who called us here, so I guess it's only fair that I start.

'Welcome to the first meeting of the Anti-Princess Club,' I say. 'Chloe and I got the idea for a club from Yiayia. Do you like the name?'

They all squeal at once: 'YESSSSSSS!'

I knew they would. I've never had an argument with any of my best friends.

Grace jumps up from her seat. 'We should have a motto,' she says. 'All the best sports clubs have mottos.'

I think back to our conversation yesterday when Bella complained about how unfair it was that princesses in fairytales always needed to be rescued by princes.

'Well, we're not a sports club,' I say. 'But how about "We Don't Need Rescuing"?'

'Yes!' they all squeal again.

I pull out my pencil and notepad.

The Anti-Princess Club:
We Don't Need Rescuing
Missions

Chloe peers over my shoulder. 'What does "Missions" mean?' she asks.

'You know how Yiayia said the friends in her club helped each other solve their problems?' I ask. 'I thought we could do the same. We could set missions to complete together.'

Bella pumps her fists. 'Yes!' she says. 'What should our first mission be?'

I pace around the picnic table just like yesterday.

'Anti-princesses,' I say, 'my mum is entering Ava and me in a beauty pageant.'

I watch them all shudder. A contest based on prettiness? Everyone knows my awesome talent is maths. Mum should be entering me in a long division, multiplication or geometry contest.

But a beauty pageant? Talk about spew-worthy.

'So, what can we do?' Grace asks. 'Do you want us to get you out of the pageant?'

'I was thinking more along the lines of a protest,' I say. 'You know, so we could take a stand against parading girls around like dolls.'

Grace nods slowly. 'Whoa, that's big. It could take a lot of planning.'

I may have hit the anti-princesses with a mission idea that's too intense to be our very first.

'Let's think about that one for a bit,' I say. 'Does anyone else have a mission they'd like to propose?'

Bella, Grace and Chloe's hands shoot up.

The pageant plotting will have to wait.

CHAPTER NINE

Bella slides a piece of
paper out of a folder in
her backpack.

She's sketched an
epic treehouse with the
letters HQ underneath.

'I drew this as soon as
I got your email last
night, Emily,' she says.

H.Q.

'I figured we'd need a club headquarters – that's
what the HQ stands for – and I've always wanted
to design a treehouse.'

Chloe, Grace and I clap with approval.

'My parents won't mind if I build it at my place,' Bella says. 'We've got the perfect tree in the backyard.'

I open my notepad and scribble underneath our club name and motto.

Mission HQ:
Build Anti-Princess clubhouse

I flip the pad around so Bella, Grace and Chloe can read it. 'All in favour?' I ask.

We all raise our hands.

Grace keeps her arm in the air. 'I have another mission to propose,' she says. 'I want to enter the Junior District Athletics Carnival.'

I should've guessed that would be Grace's wish.

We all went along to last year's carnival when Grace was too young to enter, and I still remember the look on her face when she watched the sprinters rip through the ribbon at the end of the track.

'I haven't asked Mum and Dad if I can enter yet,' she says. 'I don't want to give them any excuse to say no.'

I scratch my chin, concentrating. 'What excuse might they find?'

Grace shrugs. 'There's no ballet that day, I've already checked. And the oval is walking distance from home, so it won't be hard to get to.'

My mind switches to numbers. 'What about the money? The poster we saw at the bus stop said it was forty dollars to enter.'

Grace headbutts the table. 'Of course,' she says. 'My parents will say they don't have that sort of money and they already spend so much on ballet.' Her bottom lip trembles.

'Chin up,' I say. 'We'll think of something.'

I start doing the sums in my head. 'The carnival is in eight days, right? So we need to raise five dollars a day between now and then.'

Bella looks at me hopefully. 'That's nothing!'

'We can do that easily,' Chloe agrees.

I'm glad the girls are so enthusiastic, but I don't know how we'll raise the money. None of us plays a musical instrument, so we can't busk, and it's illegal to beg. I don't think Grace will be allowed to compete in the Olympics one day if she has a criminal record.

'We need to sell something,' I say. 'But what?'

Right on cue, Chloe pulls a lunch box out of her bag.

'Baklava!' I say. 'Chloe, you're brilliant!'

'What are you talking about?' Chloe asks. She offers the container around and we all take a piece.

'This is it, Chloe!' I say through a mouthful. 'This is edible gold.'

I can almost hear the cogs and wheels turning in Chloe's brain as she realises what I'm suggesting.

'You want me to sell my baklava to raise money for Grace's carnival?' she asks. 'But where would we sell it?'

I tap my fingers on the picnic table. 'Right here at school! We'll make a mint. Trust the mathematician here, will you?'

I do some more sums in my head. 'If we're selling at school, we need to subtract two days to account for the weekend,' I say. 'So that means we'll have six days, not eight, and we'll have to raise six dollars and sixty-seven cents per day.'

Bella counts on her fingers as she tries to follow my calculations. 'That's still doable.'

'Let's round it up to seven dollars per day,' I say. 'Because I'd like to price the baklava at seventy cents per piece.'

I flip to the next page in my notepad and start scrawling.

Mission Baklava: Raise money for Grace's carnival entry.

'All in favour?' I ask.

Everyone's hands shoot up just in the nick of time.

Briiiiing, briiiiing. Briiiiing. Briiiiing.

Recess, and our first official meeting, is over.

'What about missions to help you and me, Emily?' Chloe asks.

I shove my notepad back in my bag.

'We can't propose four missions at every meeting,' I say. 'We'll just have to be patient.'

CHAPTER TEN

The anti-princesses don't waste any time.

The final bell rings and we all meet at the school gate so we can walk back to Chloe's place and get started on the baklava.

Yiayia almost jumps out of her skin when the four of us arrive together.

'How wonderful to have you all here,' she says. 'Come and I'll make you some tea.'

Chloe hugs her. 'Don't bother with the tea, Yiayia,' she says. 'We're going to be very busy for the next little while. We need to make a batch of baklava to sell at school tomorrow.'

We follow Chloe into the kitchen and stop, startled. Chloe's mum and dad are unloading groceries into the fridge. They're usually in the restaurant at this time of day.

'What's this about selling baklava at school?' Chloe's mum asks.

Grace steps in. 'I'm fundraising to help with the cost of entering the Junior District Athletics Carnival,' she says. 'Chloe volunteered to make some baklava to sell at school. She really is such a good friend – and it's great of you to let us use your kitchen and stuff.'

Chloe's dad frowns. He's protective of his kitchen. I think he's worried about people stealing his recipes or something.

'It will be great publicity for the restaurant,' Bella says. 'When everyone gets a taste of your baklava you'll have people lining up for tables.'

Bella is so good at thinking on her feet. Surely the thought of extra business will get Chloe's parents on side.

'Hmmmm,' Chloe's dad mumbles. 'Okay, girls. Chloe could use some practice in the kitchen anyway.'

'Not if the anti-princesses have anything to do with it,' I whisper in Chloe's ear.

Chloe smiles. But now isn't the time to think about working in the restaurant kitchen. It's time to focus on cooking for Grace's mission.

Yiayia turns on the oven and Chloe starts to delegate.

'Grace, you juice the lemons and oranges,' she says. 'Bella, you grind the cloves. Emily, you crush the nuts.'

Yiayia starts flattening the pastry into tissue-thin sheets with a rolling pin while Chloe stirs the syrup on the stovetop.

'Try to juice those oranges fast, Grace,' Yiayia says quietly. 'They're Chloe's special addition. Her baba will be cross if he finds out she has meddled with the family recipe.

He thinks it's perfect the way it is.'

Grace follows Yiayia's advice and squeezes the oranges so quickly it's like she's in some sort of juicing race.

'While the baklava cools, we should head to my place,' Bella says. 'I want everyone to check out the tree where our headquarters will go.'

Yiayia chuckles. 'So much to do in one afternoon, *paidia mou*,' she says.

We're working in such perfect sync that our first tray of baklava is in the oven in no time.

'We'll get at least ten big pieces from that tray,' I say. 'And if we sell them all tomorrow for seventy cents each we'll have our first seven dollars for Grace's entry fee.'

Grace claps her hands.

Yiayia puts a crocheted tea-cosy on the pot and we all take a seat at the kitchen table. 'So how did you clever girls come up with this idea?' she asks with a knowing glint in her eye.

Chloe and I smile at each other as Yiayia places china teacups and saucers in front of us.

'It's actually thanks to you, Yiayia,' Chloe says. 'When you told Emily and me about the club you were in when you were a girl, we got the idea to start our own.'

Yiayia puffs out her chest and rolls her shoulders back. I think I even see a tear on her cheek. She looks super pleased to be the one who inspired the club.

'And this is your first duty?' she asks. 'Baking to raise money for Grace?'

We all nod as we sip our tea.

'We're called the Anti-Princess Club,' I say. 'Our motto is "We Don't Need Rescuing".'

Yiayia laughs. 'Princesses you girls are not,' she says. 'Talented and independent, yes; princesses, no. That doesn't mean you aren't all beautiful, though. I miss the days when I was as pretty as you.'

If it wasn't Yiayia commenting on the way we look I would roll my eyes, but I don't want to be disrespectful. We all love Yiayia and she really does understand us.

'Speaking of beauty,' I say, 'that's another mission ahead of us. We need to think of a way to get me out of the beauty pageant. Maybe we can hold some sort of protest against girls being judged on their prettiness before pageant day.'

Grace adds honey to her chamomile tea. 'I know a bit about pageants,' she says. 'When I have a ballet performance Mum makes me wear a little bit of make-up because apparently the stage lights make your face look dull. But some of the other girls also enter beauty pageants. They spend hours getting ready – curling their hair and slopping loads of make-up on their faces. Then they have to parade around in a sparkly dress in front of some judges. The judges choose who they think is the prettiest and she gets a tiara.'

Yiayia furrows her brow and makes a 'hmmmmmm' sound. I hope we haven't offended her. I hope she doesn't like the idea of beauty pageants.

'You should enter the pageant, Emily,' Yiayia says.

I drop my teacup in shock. Hot tea splatters over the floor. I jump up from my seat to look for something to clean up the mess.

'Is anyone burnt?' I ask. 'Did I splash anyone?'

Everyone shakes their heads reassuringly.

'Don't worry, I'll fix the mess, *paidi mou*,'

Yiayia says, motioning for me to sit back down. 'But the pageant – if you have a point to make, you won't make it by not turning up. You need to be onstage.'

I pick up my empty teacup and compose myself. I don't agree with Yiayia. If I enter the pageant I won't be defending my beliefs. I'll be giving in to Mum and Hungry and their eyebrow-plucking, starving ways.

'Go in the pageant, Emily – but don't wear any make-up or a fancy dress,' Yiayia continues. 'Show them who you really are and be proud.'

The anti-princesses nod.

'Yiayia's right,' Chloe says. 'You could make a speech onstage about why beauty pageants are unfair.'

Now I understand where Yiayia is coming from. She doesn't want me to enter the pageant as a regular competitor. She wants me to use my entry to take a stand against the craziness of judging girls on their looks.

Yiayia's won me over. It is a brilliant plan. It's a plan that's going to get me into a lot of trouble with Mum and Hungry, but it's brilliant all the same.

I grab my notepad out of my backpack and pull out a pencil. I can't believe I'm about to write these words.

Mission Tiara:
Become undercover beauty queen
to protest against pageant

CHAPTER ELEVEN

'Are you ready?' Bella asks.

It's time for her to unveil the blueprint for the Anti-Princess Club headquarters. It didn't take her long to finish the design. When she's really excited about something, the sketches flow out of her fingers.

Grace, Chloe and I are sitting underneath a tall eucalypt in Bella's backyard. Max and the babysitter, Louis, are inside watching a movie – Bella told them to leave us alone out here so she could make her special presentation.

'This is the tree we'll build the treehouse in,'

Bella says. 'I've already hammered some pieces of wood to the trunk so we can climb up to the first set of branches. That's where the first storey will be. Then, there will be a few more steps to the second storey.'

Grace can't contain herself. 'A *two*-storey treehouse?! You're amazing, Bella!'

Bella keeps a straight face and continues her presentation. She's taking it very seriously, because she's imagining we're wealthy investors who want her to build us a real-life version of her icypole-stick hotel.

'The second storey is where you'll find the biggest part of the treehouse,' Bella says. 'That will be a simple room with four walls, two windows and a roof. Inside the roof will be another tiny space where we can hide anything we need to keep secret.'

The mention of a secret space sends us all into a round of squeals. Bella is pleased we're so excited, but keeps her composure.

'I can't wait to start building it, Bella,' Chloe says. 'But where will we get all the materials?'

Bella hasn't figured that bit out yet, so she tries to distract us from the question. 'Let me demonstrate how easy it is to climb the ladder.'

We watch as Bella climbs the steps.

At the sixth step I start to worry. She's very high up. I call out, 'It's getting dark, Bella. Be careful!'

As Bella turns to yell back at me, the sixth step breaks and falls out from underneath her. There's nowhere for her to put her feet.

She tries to grab a branch above her head, but it's just out of reach. There's nothing to hold on to. It all happens in a split second, but it looks as if her body is falling backwards in slow motion.

'Bella!' I scream.

Bella lands on the ground with a thud.

Grace, Chloe and I leap to our feet and

surround her. She
tries to lift her head
as we hover over her,
but she can't do it.

'Bella, can you
hear me?' Chloe asks.

There's no answer.

I pull Bella's hair off
her face and see a smear of
red across her forehead. Grace
takes a hanky out of her pocket
and starts wiping it away.

Bella opens her eyes into a squint.

'Gross,' she mutters. 'Get that spew-worthy
hanky away from my face.'

We're too worried to laugh.

'You're bleeding, Bella,' I say.

I'm about to call out to Max and Louis
when we're blinded by the headlights of a car
pulling up in the driveway.

'It's Bella's dad,' Chloe says.

The car door closes and Grace calls out, 'Down here, Dr MacKenzie! There's been an accident!'

Bella's dad has a different surname to the rest of the family, and he and Dr Singh have always been too busy to get married.

Dr MacKenzie drops a pile of folders and starts running across the backyard, still in his white doctor's coat.

'She fell out of the tree,' I say when he reaches us. 'We're building a treehouse.'

Dr MacKenzie bends down. He checks if she can move her neck. She can.

He holds up four fingers in front of Bella's face. 'How many?'

'Four,' she says.

Dr MacKenzie takes a deep breath and smiles softly. He examines her forehead.

'Looks like you've had quite a bump,' he says. 'Your face is okay. The blood is coming from a cut on your head. The good news is this cut isn't very deep. You won't need stitches.'

We're so lucky Bella's dad is a doctor.

The deck light comes on and Louis cranes his neck around the back door.

'What's going on out here?' he calls.

Dr MacKenzie picks Bella up and mutters quietly, 'What a great babysitter you've got there.'

'Don't blame him,' I whisper. 'We told him to stay inside with Max. He didn't know about the treehouse.'

We follow Bella and her dad to the house.

Louis and Max gasp as we pass them at the back door and they see the bloody hanky pressed to Bella's head.

'Cool!' Max says.

Dr MacKenzie takes Bella into the lounge room and lays her down on the couch. He looks at her head again.

'She's going to be okay,' he tells us. 'I'll have to keep an eye on her, though. She might have a mild concussion.'

Louis starts sobbing. 'It's all my fault. I'm so sorry.'

'It's not your fault,' Dr MacKenzie says reassuringly. 'Apparently my little princess thought it would be a good idea to get a little wild and climb a tree.'

'*Aaaaaaahhhhhhhhhh!*'

Bella's scream is not a scream of pain. It's a scream of frustration.

'Dad, I am not a princess!' she yells. 'I don't even *like* them!'

The front door clicks shut. Bella's mum is home.

'What is wrong with your head, Bella?' she asks. 'And what do you mean, you don't like princesses?'

Poor Dr Singh. Bella didn't want her mum to find out about her princess hatred like this. She wanted to break it to her gently.

'I've never liked princesses, Mum,' she says. 'I didn't have the heart to tell you.'

Dr Singh inhales deeply as she digests Bella's words. Then she exhales and leans over Bella to examine her forehead. 'Are you sure that's not a concussion talking?'

Bella sits up and looks directly into her mum's eyes. 'I'm sorry, Mum,' she says. 'You too, Dad. I just want to design and build stuff. That's what I was doing out there. I'm going to build a treehouse.'

Dr MacKenzie spots the treehouse blueprint on the floor. I pick it up and pass it to him.

'I think it's time for you girls to head home,' he says. 'Bella, you'll need to take the day off school tomorrow. And if you're feeling better, it looks like we have a treehouse to build.'

CHAPTER TWELVE

It's our first money-making day. It's recess, and Chloe is armed with a container full of her edible gold.

With Bella staying home with her suspected concussion, Chloe, Grace and I will have to work extra hard as salespeople.

I cross my fingers and toes that the mission works.

'Here's the plan,' I say. 'Grace and I will take three pieces of baklava each and Chloe will take four. Then I'll head to the soccer field, Grace, you take the basketball court and

Chloe, you target the area outside the library. The baklava is seventy cents a piece. No less. If anyone tries to argue with the price, send them to the canteen where the cheapest snack is a whole dollar. They'll soon figure out where to find the better deal.'

The anti-princesses don't seem to mind me taking over the mission. I'm not just the club founder, I'm also a mathematician. When it comes to money, you want someone like me in charge.

Chloe divides up the baklava and puts it onto three paper plates. I hand out envelopes for the money with a few coins inside in case anyone needs change.

'Any questions?' I ask.

Grace and Chloe shake their heads.

'Good,' I say. 'Let's get this mission going.'

We take off to our separate parts of the playground.

I call out, 'Fresh baklava! Get your baklava

here! Only seventy cents a piece!'

A couple of boys from third grade run over. They scan the baklava with suspicion. One gives it a sniff.

'What is bark lover?' he asks. 'It looks gross.'

'It sounds like something tree huggers eat,' the other one jokes.

I didn't expect this trouble. All the anti-princesses love Chloe's baklava. Besides, it doesn't look gross, just different. And that bark-lover-tree-hugger joke was lame.

'It's sticky pastry filled with nuts,' I say. 'I know it doesn't look like a normal recess treat, like a lamington or a cupcake, but it's really yummy. It's from Greece. You should try it.'

One of the boys hands over seventy cents and takes a slice. He turns it upside down to look at the bottom. Eventually he takes a bite and slowly begins to chew.

'Not bad,' he says. 'Did you make it?'

'My friend Chloe made it — her family owns

the Greek restaurant in town,' I say. 'You can buy a second piece if you want.'

The boy buys another piece. His friend hesitates, then also pulls seventy cents out of his pocket.

'I just ate a pie so I'm not really hungry,' he says. 'But I guess I can take it home and try it later.'

Before I can stash the money I've raised, a row of at least ten kids has lined up.

'I'm sorry, I don't have any more,' I say. 'But my friends are selling some on the other side of the playground.'

A sixth-grade boy at the back of the line

calls out, 'I just tried to buy some from that blonde girl, but she's all out of it too.'

I don't want to disappoint the crowd. We're going to need their money tomorrow and for another five days after that. I think fast.

'If you come back tomorrow we'll have double the amount of baklava,' I blurt out. 'That's a promise.'

The sixth-grader grunts. How rude. I poke my tongue out behind his back.

I head back to the picnic tables. The other anti-princesses arrive at the same time.

'I was mobbed,' Grace says. 'The plate was empty in seconds.'

Chloe looks pooped. She wipes her forehead on her arm and looks at her watch. 'You know, I'm glad to be helping Grace with all this baking,' she says. 'But I think it's time to propose a mission for myself.'

I take out my notepad in anticipation.

'I want to win the science fair,' Chloe says.

'I want to show Mum and Dad that I belong in a lab coat, not an apron.'

I think Chloe's mission could be the most simple of all – she's the best scientist in school by far.

Mission Lab Coat:
Help Chloe win science fair.

'All in favour?' I ask.

Grace, Chloe and I raise our hands.

Now that I've got Chloe in a good mood, I decide to break the news to her about my promise to the sixth-graders.

'Soooooooooo,' I say. 'Do you think it would be possible to make double the amount of baklava this afternoon?'

CHAPTER THIRTEEN

We arrive at Chloe's apartment and immediately go into baking mode. Yiayia has already preheated the oven and placed the ingredients on the kitchen table.

'Thank you, Yiayia, but we're going to need more,' Chloe says. 'We're making double.'

I start counting cinnamon sticks and cloves while the rest of the anti-princesses tie their apron strings.

'You know, this could work out for the best,' I say. 'I originally did my sums based on six days of sales. If we can sell double the amount of baklava we can halve the number of days we need to sell it.'

Knock, knock, knock. Knock. Knock.

Someone is knocking on the restaurant door downstairs.

'Must be an impatient customer,' Yiayia says. 'The restaurant is not open for another two hours.'

The knock gets louder. *Knock, knock, knock. Knock. KNOCK.*

Chloe opens a window and peers out at the street below.

'The restaurant is closed,' she calls out. 'Come back later.'

She's about to shut the window when we hear a man's voice yell back.

'I need to speak to the pastry chef!'

I freeze. Something must have gone wrong. Maybe someone at school had an allergic reaction. Maybe someone was in trouble for spending all their lunch money. Maybe it was a teacher angry at us because we didn't ask permission to sell the baklava in the playground.

'What should I do?' Chloe asks.

Yiayia shakes her finger at Chloe. 'You're not going downstairs alone. Not to see a stranger.'

Grace and I speak at once. 'We'll come too.'

The three of us make our way downstairs and Chloe slowly peeks around the door to where the man is waiting.

'I made the baklava,' she says. 'What do you want?'

The man is holding a half-eaten piece.

'I've never tasted anything like it,' he says. 'There's something different about it. It's not like the baklava I've had in this restaurant before.'

'It's my own secret recipe,' Chloe says. 'It's not the same as the baklava Mum and Dad sell. Do you want to buy a piece? We sell it at school.'

The man shoves the rest of the piece in his mouth and swallows it in almost one gulp. Like a python.

'I know you've been selling it at school,' he says. 'My son brought it home. But I don't want to buy just a piece. I want to buy the recipe.'

The mention of money spurs me into action. I put my hands on my hips. 'Oh, yeah? How much are you willing to pay?'

The man takes a piece of paper and a fancy pen from his shirt pocket. He scribbles something and folds the paper in half. He hands it to me. It's all very official.

I take a look at the paper. It must be a mistake.

The man reads my mind. 'I'm not messing around. That's what I'm willing to pay.'

I start fanning myself with the paper. 'We'll have to discuss this with Chloe's parents,' I say. 'They will be in touch at a later date.'

I take the man's business card with his phone number and quickly usher the anti-princesses back inside.

'What does it say, Emily?' asks Chloe.

'Fifty dollars!' I squeal. 'He wants to pay you *fifty dollars*, Chloe. I've never even touched a fifty-dollar note!'

Chloe snatches the paper from my hand. She stares at it for one, two, three, four seconds.

'This can't be right,' she says.

I nod excitedly. 'I think it is, Chloe,' I say. 'It's for real.'

'Well, you're correct,' Chloe says. 'I will definitely need to speak to my parents about this.'

She runs back upstairs, holding the paper above her head. Grace and I follow, busting to spill the news to Yiayia.

'What happened, girls?' Yiayia asks. 'Who was that man?'

I figure it's Chloe's story to tell. It could be the story of the decade, or the century, or the millennium.

'The man wanted my baklava recipe,' Chloe says. 'His son took a piece home from school and the man tasted it. He liked it so much that he wants to know how I made it.'

She's forgetting the most important part. The number part.

'He wants to *buy* the recipe, Yiayia,' I say. 'For *fifty* dollars. Chloe could be rich!'

Yiayia drops a wooden spoon. 'Who would spend that on a recipe?' she asks. 'It must be some kind of joke.'

Chloe shows her the piece of paper. 'This is what he's offering, Yiayia. Maybe he wants my recipe so he can sell the baklava too.'

I chime in, 'Maybe he owns a business, like a factory where he could make masses of baklava.'

Grace yelps and points at the doorway to the apartment.

The man is standing inside with Chloe's mum and dad.

They're all staring at us. Chloe's parents look confused.

'This man was outside the restaurant,' Chloe's mum says. 'He tells us he wants to buy our baklava recipe.'

Chloe's dad's face reddens. 'But he says it's not the same as the baklava from the restaurant.'

Chloe swallows loudly. 'It's a...it's a...it's a secret recipe,' she blurts out. 'I did some experimenting. It's not very different to yours, Dad. Just a few extra ingredients. That's all.'

Chloe's dad looks at me for a moment. He looks at the other anti-princesses.

'I think you girls need to leave,' he says. 'We must speak to our daughter privately.'

CHAPTER FOURTEEN

Bella, Grace and I are sitting on the first floor of our new clubhouse.

When Chloe's dad turfed us out, Grace and I decided to go and check on the new headquarters. And Bella's head, of course.

So far, HQ is just a wooden platform. It does have a solid set of steps now, though.

'What do you think, girls?' Dr MacKenzie calls out from underneath the tree. 'Bella and I have had a great time today on the tools.'

Bella grins. She's never built anything with her dad before.

'It's looking great, Dr MacKenzie,' I say. 'You'll be finished in no time.'

Bella's dad climbs a few steps so he doesn't have to yell. 'I reckon we'll be done by the end of the week. Mostly thanks to Bella, mind you. I don't know where you get your impressive building skills from, princess.'

Bella winces.

'Sorry, sorry,' her dad says. 'I forgot about the princess thing. I won't call you that anymore.' He takes a few more steps up and ruffles Bella's hair. 'Thanks again for a wonderful day. It'll be hard to go back to work tomorrow.'

He heads inside to give us some privacy.

'So are you okay, Bella?' I ask.

She runs her fingers over her forehead. 'I can't even feel the bump anymore. I'm totally fine. Better than fine. I'm awesome. So, where's Chloe?'

Grace lets out a long sigh. 'She's in trouble and it's all because of me,' she says. 'No one would have ever found out about Chloe's baklava if we weren't selling it at school. The whole mission was for me.'

Bella raises one eyebrow. I wish I could do that, but both seem to move at once. 'Why exactly is Chloe in trouble?'

I sum it up as best I can. 'A stranger got a hold of Chloe's baklava and loved it so much he wanted to buy the recipe for fifty whole dollars. But then Chloe's parents found out she'd messed with the restaurant recipe and they weren't happy.'

Bella whistles. 'Wow, that could pay for your carnival entry, Grace. No baklava baking.'

Grace shakes her head. 'No, I couldn't take it. That wouldn't be completing the mission. And what would Chloe's parents say? We've still got time to fundraise for me.'

I cross my legs and slump forward with my chin resting on my hands.

'Do you think the club was a bad idea?' I ask. 'It's barely been twenty-four hours and Chloe is in trouble with her parents. Grace, we haven't raised all the money for your carnival, and Bella, you fell out of a tree.'

Bella stands up in a huff. She starts marching around the platform. It's exactly what I do when we're at the picnic tables at school and I want to make a point.

'Anti-princesses, you're being silly,' she says. 'We don't need rescuing, remember?'

Grace and I both give her a half-smile.

'The headquarters are already half-finished,' Bella says. 'Mission HQ will be complete soon enough, but it wouldn't have happened so fast if it wasn't for Dad's help. And you know what? Dad wouldn't have helped me if it wasn't for you. He and Mum would still be coming home from the hospital late at night, not knowing anything about my building or art skills. Now they know the real me. It's all because of the Anti-Princess Club.'

Our half-smiles have turned into full-on beams. I stand up and give Bella a hug.

'Great speech, Bella,' I say. 'You might have to help me with my big performance at the beauty pageant.'

Bella laughs. 'Oh, we're all going to have to pitch in for that one,' she says. 'Getting you through a beauty pageant without wanting to spew is going to be one *big* mission.'

CHAPTER FIFTEEN

It's time to lie to my mum. I'm not a good liar and I don't like lying. But an anti-princess does what an anti-princess must do.

Luckily, there's one part of this lie that makes it easier. It's a lie that's going to make Mum happy...at least for a while.

I knock on her bedroom door.

'Come in,' she calls.

Mum is sitting at her dressing table cleaning her face. She takes a white fluffy cottonwool ball and wipes it across her cheek. The ball ends up brown and sticky.

'Mum, you look better without make-up,' I say.

She rolls her eyes. 'Emily, do we really have to have this conversation again? I love make-up – it makes me feel beautiful.'

The moment is here.

'It's funny you should mention beauty,' I say. 'I've been thinking about that pageant.'

Mum begins to collect the brown cottonwool balls scattered around her dressing table. 'I know, I know, Emily. You don't want to do it.'

I help her pick up the balls. They feel slimy. 'That's the thing,' I say. 'I ... do ... want ... to ... go ... in ... the ... pageant.'

There it is. The lie.

Mum drops her handful of brown balls. Before I can protest, she lifts me up and spins me around until we can hardly stand. Then the kisses start coming. *Kiss, kiss. Kiss. Kiss.*

'Enough, Mum, enough,' I laugh. 'It's no big deal. I just want to try something new. That's all.'

Mum walks into her wardrobe and comes out with a big pink box.

'I couldn't resist buying this,' she says. 'Even though I thought you'd say no to the pageant. I figured Ava could have it later on if you didn't want it.'

I open the box and pull out the frilliest, sparkliest, pouffiest dress I've ever seen. It's bright yellow. It's so bright that it's almost painful to look at – like when you try to look directly into a fire, or the sun.

'You have to try it on,' Mum says. 'Please, Emily.'

There's nothing I want to do less. But if Mum's going to believe I truly want to go in the pageant, I have to put that awful thing on. I step into the mass of frills.

'Be careful,' Mum says. 'There are lots of beads and sequins on the fabric. Make sure you don't pull anything off.'

It must be so difficult for pageant contestants. They'd be constantly stressed about losing a bead. They wouldn't be able to run or climb. It would even be difficult to sit.

Mum pulls the dress up over my tummy and starts to fasten the zip, which pinches some skin between my shoulderblades.

'Ouch!' I cry.

'Don't be sooky, Emily,' she says. 'Beauty is painful.'

That, I think to myself, is exactly what the anti-princesses are fighting against and why I have to pull off this mission. There are so many more important things in life than prettiness. And girls definitely shouldn't have to hurt themselves to look good.

CHAPTER SIXTEEN

There's no answer when I knock on Chloe's door the next morning to see if she wants to walk to school with me.

So I walk alone, nervously counting in my head the whole way.

We won't have any baklava to sell today and I promised that sixth grader we would have double. I don't know when, or even if, we'll have any more baklava to sell for Grace's carnival. I fear our mission is doomed.

I arrive at the school gate and see Chloe waiting for me. Her smile is as big as a quarter of a watermelon. Weird – I thought she would be as worried as me.

'What's going on?' I ask.

Chloe pulls four large containers out of a canvas shopping bag. 'Surprise!'

I do a double-take. Then a triple-take. And a quadruple-take.

'How is this possible?' I ask. 'Chloe, this must have taken forever.'

Some boys see the baklava and start milling around us.

'Don't thank me,' Chloe says. 'Thank Yiayia. She stayed up late baking. She knew how important this fundraising was to the club.'

I'm amazed. Yiayia is wicked. I hope I'm as cool as she is when I'm seventy-eight.

'What happened when we left your place?' I ask. 'Are you in much trouble with your parents?'

'Don't worry about me,' Chloe says. 'Mum and Dad sent me to my room so they could talk to the man about my recipe. They didn't seem too excited, so I'm guessing they didn't take the money. They said they were too busy in the restaurant to talk to me and that they'll sit down with me after school today.'

I give Chloe a hug. She deserved that fifty dollars.

'It's okay, because I had time to start building my diorama for the science fair,' Chloe says. 'I'm making the planets out of fruit. Mars is a lychee, Jupiter's a melon and Neptune's a lime. Lychees aren't actually in season, but the restaurant's fruit supplier organised to get me one from a batch imported from Thailand.'

Ms Bayliss is on playground duty and she spots us at the school gate. She looks at us and the boys loitering around the containers.

'You must be the famous baklava sellers I've been hearing so much about,' she calls out. 'Make sure you tell your customers that baklava contains nuts. I don't fancy confiscating your produce because you've sold it to someone with an allergy.'

Ms Bayliss is pretty awesome. I didn't think we would be in trouble for selling the baklava – it is for a good cause. But the thought of having Yiayia's massive cooking efforts confiscated is scary.

We get to class and Bella immediately draws up four signs to stick on each batch of baklava:

Warning, contains nuts!

...ns nuts!

The anti-princesses make a few more sales in class. I try not to giggle as I watch Chloe pass a piece of baklava under the desk to Violet in the back row.

We break for recess and walk to the picnic tables. Bella and Grace are with me, but Chloe's staying behind to pick up an entry form for the science fair.

I start dividing the baklava between us so we can sell it in the playground.

Before I'm done, Chloe bounds around the corner towards us. She's running almost as fast as Grace. Her face is as red as a tomato.

'Stop, stop!' she yells.

'What is it?' I ask. 'Is something wrong?'

Chloe tries to speak, but she's too out of breath. 'I … I just … it's amazing … I just …' she huffs and puffs.

Grace gently grabs Chloe by the shoulders and looks her in the eye. 'I saw Dad do this to one of my brothers at a soccer match once,' she says. 'Calm down. Take a deep breath and tell us what you're trying to say.'

Chloe ignores the advice and starts jumping up and down like a pogo stick.

'Give the baklava away!' she shrieks. 'Give it away for free! I was just talking to the boy whose dad wanted to buy the recipe. He told me it's done! They did the deal last night! We're going to be rich!'

It certainly is awesome news. I can see why Chloe is overwhelmed, but we still need to raise the money for Grace's carnival.

'Don't you see, Grace?' asks Chloe. 'I can give you the money for your carnival. We don't have to waste any more time baking and selling this baklava. Frankly, I'm sick of it! It's been baklava this, baklava that. I've had enough baklava to last a lifetime!'

Bella and I start laughing and jumping up and down with Chloe.

'I can give you the money for your carnival ... I can give you the money for your carnival.' Grace repeats Chloe's sentence over and over. 'Wait a minute. Are you sure your parents will let you give me the money?'

Chloe nods excitedly. 'Of course,' she says. 'It is *my* recipe. The buyer wouldn't have even tasted the baklava if it wasn't for us selling it at school for your carnival.'

Grace holds up her hands for us to stop celebrating.

'No, you can't do it, Chloe,' she says. 'We'd be failing our mission, which was to bake the baklava and sell it. We have to follow through.'

I admire Grace's dedication, but I think I can find a loophole. I pull my notepad from my backpack and flip to the page where I first wrote down our mission to help Grace.

'Here it is,' I say. 'You're wrong, Grace. Our mission never mentioned baking baklava. I wrote it right here – see?'

Mission Baklava: Raise money
for Grace's carnival entry.

'So, what you're saying is, it doesn't matter *how* we raised the money?' Grace asks.

'Exactly!' I squeal. 'The method wasn't important. Just the result. All we had to do was find the money. And it's done!'

Grace finally gives in to the excitement and starts jumping too. 'Free baklava for everyone!' she yells. 'Come and take it! First in, first served!'

A stampede of sixth-graders almost knocks us over as they run for the picnic tables. We scoot out of the way as they fight for the pieces like squawking seagulls competing for hot chips at the beach. In the blink of an eye, the plates are empty.

The sixth-grader I made the promise to yesterday folds his arms and stomps his feet. 'Hey, I didn't get any,' he whines. 'You have to make more.'

'Make it yourself,' I say. 'We've got better things to do than cook for boys.'

CHAPTER SEVENTEEN

It has quite possibly been the most exciting day of our lives.

We're on a high. As Chloe and I walk home from school it almost feels as though we're floating.

'If I could bottle up a formula to recreate this feeling I would definitely win a Nobel Prize,' Chloe says. 'It would be a potion to make you weightless. An anti-gravity serum. There are so many scientific possibilities.'

We arrive at Chloe's apartment and the sight of her brother eating fruit salad brings us back to earth. Seeing Alex reminds us of Chloe's dilemma: working in the restaurant.

Her mum and dad still haven't told her when she will have to start. And Chloe still hasn't had the guts to ask.

'What's the matter, Chloe?' Alex asks. 'Shouldn't you be pretty chuffed right now?'

He has obviously heard about the recipe deal.

'I'm giving it to Grace,' Chloe says. 'I don't care about earning any money. That's why I'd rather have my weekends to myself than work in the restaurant kitchen.'

Alex scratches his head. 'Hang on,' he says. 'I thought you'd like it there, being surrounded by all that baking. You love cooking, don't you? You created that baklava recipe.'

Chloe looks frustrated, so I interrupt.

'It's not the cooking she likes,' I say. 'It's the mixing, the experimenting, the coming up with new concoctions.'

He still doesn't get it.

'It's the *science*, Alex,' I explain. 'Chloe loves science.'

Alex spoons some more fruit salad into his mouth. 'Well, Professor Chloe, you better tell Mum and Dad you don't want to work in the kitchen,' he says between mouthfuls. 'They're counting on you for next Saturday. I saw your name on the roster.'

Chloe's eyes narrow. 'Where did you get the lychee in that fruit salad, Alex?'

Alex swallows. 'It was in a box on the coffee table,' he says. 'There was a lime and a honeydew melon too. Want some?'

Chloe freaks. She launches herself at Alex and starts pounding his chest with her fists.

'No, no, no!' she cries. 'First you get a scholarship to boarding school, then I have to work in the restaurant on weekends, and now you eat my science fair project!'

Alex shields himself from Chloe's swinging arms. 'Eat your project? What are you on about?'

Yiayia and Chloe's parents rush into the lounge room from the stairwell.

Tears are flowing down Chloe's cheeks. I help Yiayia pull her away from her brother.

We're all in a state of shock. We've never seen Chloe behave that way.

'Everyone calm down,' Chloe's mum says. 'Can someone explain what's going on here?'

The moment has finally arrived. 'The talk' is coming. Chloe's weekends are about to be made a thing of the past.

I wonder if I should leave, but Yiayia motions for me to take a seat.

I sit with Chloe and her mum and dad on the couch. Yiayia and Alex head to the kitchen to pour some tea.

'Alex's fruit salad was supposed to be my science project,' Chloe says. 'And I don't want to work in the kitchen when Alex leaves. I don't want to be a dishwasher. I don't even want to be a cook. I'm a scientist.'

Chloe's dad surprises us all with his response.

'Okay,' he says.

Chloe wipes her eyes. 'What do you mean, *okay*?'

'Chloe, a scientist needs to check her facts,' her dad says.

Yiayia and Alex bring in teacups, but I can't drink. I'm too anxious to hear what facts Chloe hasn't checked.

'We were never going to force you to work in the restaurant, Chloe,' her mum says. 'We thought you might like to help with the lunch rush for an hour or so on Saturdays. That's why we put your name down to replace your brother, but it's not set in stone.'

I cover my smile with my hands.

'So, this is just a big misunderstanding?' Chloe asks.

Her dad takes a sip of tea. 'You obviously have a great talent, Chloe. One we haven't recognised before, but Yiayia has filled us in.'

'We want to use those talents,' Chloe's mum continues. 'We'd love it if you came up with more recipes – or call them experiments if you prefer. Maybe it is time we went through some of our old dishes and gave them a fresh twist.'

Chloe's lips begin to curl upwards.

'Let me get this straight,' she says. 'I don't have to work in the kitchen, or the restaurant?'

'For a science whiz, you're not a very good listener,' Alex scoffs.

'No, Chloe, you will not have to work in the restaurant or the kitchen,' her mum says. 'You're only ten. All we ask is one of your amazing recipes every once in a while.'

Chloe pounces on her mum for a hug. Then Chloe and her dad hug. Then Chloe and Yiayia hug. Then Chloe and I hug. Chloe even gives Alex a tight squeeze.

It's back to being the best day of our lives. We just need to find a fresh lychee.

CHAPTER EIGHTEEN

Bella's mum, dad, brother and all the anti-princesses are chipping in to finish the treehouse.

Dr MacKenzie hired a proper builder to get the walls up, windows in and roof on. She told Bella she was very impressed with her design.

'All we need is a coat of paint,' Bella says.

Dr MacKenzie has tins of all the primary colours ready to go.

'How about blue?' he asks. 'Blue's not too girly.'

Bella groans. Her favourite colour is actually pink, but not because she's a girl. She likes how fuschia brightens up a painting or drawing.

And she especially loves a pink sky, like at dusk.

'What's wrong, Bella?' her mum asks. 'What have we done now?'

Bella's parents have been trying hard to please her. And they're not doing it with gifts, they're doing it with time. They've actually taken a weekend off work and they're using it wisely.

'I was thinking pink might be better,' I say. 'That's Bella's favourite colour.'

Bella's parents are surprised. They just got

used to the fact Bella doesn't like fairytales and dolls.

'It's not about what's best for boys and what's best for girls,' Bella tries to explain. 'It's about everyone being different. Some girls *do* like fairytales and dolls. I suppose some boys do too.'

Max calls out from the top of the treehouse, 'Not me. No dolls for me, thank you very much.'

We all laugh.

'I guess what I'm trying to say is, you can't assume someone is going to like something or not like something,' Bella goes on. 'You need to get to know them.'

She decides to use the anti-princesses to make her point.

'You can't just assume that Chloe likes cooking because her parents own a restaurant,' she continues. 'The truth is she doesn't really like cooking. Her awesome talent is science. And Grace's mum and dad make her do ballet because they think that's what girls are good at. But Grace's awesome talent is running. And Emily…everyone talks about how pretty she is because they think that's what girls want to hear, but all Emily wants is for people to realise that her awesome talent is maths.'

Max climbs out of the treehouse and flops down on the grass. 'What's this got to do with paint?'

Dr Singh raises a finger to her lips. 'Shhhh, Max,' she says. 'Let your sister finish.'

'What's this got to do with paint?' Bella repeats. 'I want pink paint. That's what. My name is Bella, I don't like fairytales, my awesome talents are building and art, and I want to paint my treehouse pink.'

Dr MacKenzie pulls some paintbrushes out of the toolbox. 'Pink it is,' he says. 'Let's get mixing that red and white.'

Two hours later the treehouse is finished. *Mission HQ: complete.*

CHAPTER NINETEEN

Grace's mum and dad think they're at the Junior District Athletics Carnival to spectate. Grace is so close to being able to compete that she didn't want to risk her chance by telling them about her entry too soon.

Even though we've paid the entry fee, Grace hasn't been able to turn off that tiny voice in her head saying her parents could still stop her. But she has to tell them sooner or later. She just needs to find the right moment.

Bella, Chloe and I join Grace and her family in the grandstand, trying to contain our excitement so as not to reveal Grace's secret.

A group of boys walk past and Mr Bennett nods hello in their direction.

'Good runners, those boys,' he says. 'They'll be stars one day, just you watch.'

A voice booms over the loudspeaker: '*Under-eleven girls, please meet at the end of the hundred-metre track.*'

It's now or never.

Grace closes her eyes and inhales.

'Mum, Dad, I have to go and line up,' she blurts. 'I'm competing. I entered the carnival.'

Grace's mum looks at her sympathetically. 'Sweetie, you can't enter,' she says. 'It costs a lot of money.'

Money talk. This is where I shine.

'We've paid for her,' I say. 'It was forty dollars. We started fundraising at school – we planned to make six dollars and seventy cents per day, but then Chloe was given fifty dollars, so we ended up with more than enough.'

Grace's dad coughs. Or is he choking? 'You can't do something like this without our permission,' he splutters. 'You're only ten, Grace.'

Bella boldly steps forward. 'Her first race is only a few minutes away. You're not going to stop her, are you?' She pulls a rolled-up sheet of cardboard from her backpack and unravels it.

'And we baked and baked to raise money for Grace's entry fee,' adds Chloe. 'You're not going to let all our work go to waste, are you?'

Mrs Bennett smiles and runs her hand over Bella's sign. 'This is very sweet, girls,' she says. 'You've put in a lot of effort.'

She seems to have come around. The anti-princesses have worked their magic on her.

Mr Bennett, meanwhile, has not come

around. His lips are twisting into a cat's-bottom pucker and his nostrils are flaring. It's as though he's trying to think of an excuse to stop her, but he can't find the words.

'Go, Grace,' I say. 'We'll cheer you on here with your mum and dad.'

Grace runs off without looking back.

Bella, Chloe and I stand up so we can get the best possible view of the race.

Grace takes her place at the starting line.

'This is it, Grace,' I whisper. 'Everything you've been working so hard for is about to happen.'

The starting gun goes off. Grace takes her first big step. Then another, then another. *Step, step. Step. Step.*

Her legs are moving so fast they're almost detaching from her body. Her eyes are focused on the ribbon pulled across the finish line.

It seems to take only milliseconds for Grace to burst through that ribbon. Her first proper hundred-metre race is over. Just like that.

The crowd is going nuts. The anti-princesses are the loudest of all.

'Woohoo, Grace!' Chloe yells. 'Go, Grace!' I squeal. 'We love you, Grace!' cries Bella.

Grace makes the slow walk back to the grandstand.

Her dad is dumbstruck. He hasn't uttered a word since Grace left for the track.

'We knew you'd win, Grace,' I say. 'And you're going to win the next four races too.'

Grace's dad opens his mouth to speak. 'You... you beat them by half a length,' he says. 'The others...they were still at the fifty-metre mark when you broke the hundred-metre ribbon.'

'I had no idea you were so fast, Grace,' her mum says.

Her parents are pretty clueless for grown-ups. Athletics is Grace's calling. This is what we've been trying to explain to them for years.

Grace's brothers run over from the officials' desk. 'Grace, you beat the boys!' yells Oliver.

'There were no boys in that race,' their dad snorts. 'What are you talking about?'

'Her time, Dad,' Oliver says. 'We just checked it with the timekeepers. Grace was a whole second faster than the winner of the ten-year-old boys' race.'

Bella, Chloe and I leap towards Grace to give her a group hug.

'A whole second is a long time over a distance of a hundred metres,' I say. 'Trust me. I know numbers.'

I think Grace's mum is crying. I'm pretty sure they're happy tears, though. Proud, happy tears.

Her dad puts his hand on Grace's shoulder.

'I was wrong, Grace,' he says. 'You're exceptional. You won by such a distance and you beat the boys. You're a star.'

It's great to see Grace win the next four races. It's even greater to see her win over her mum and dad.

Mission Baklava: complete.

CHAPTER TWENTY

Yiayia doesn't get behind the wheel much, but when the occasion calls she drives the restaurant van. And Chloe's solar system diorama is such an occasion, so Yiayia takes her and me to the science fair.

Bella and Grace are here too. The three of us didn't bother entering the fair – we'd rather help Chloe complete her mission to win.

I spent a good two hours combing the internet for somewhere Chloe could find a new lychee. We tracked some down at an Asian grocery store on the other side of the city.

Chloe used the ten dollars she had left over from the recipe deal to buy a whole bag so she'd have back-ups.

This morning I headed over to Chloe's before school so I could measure the circumference of every piece of fruit in the diorama to make sure the ratios were perfect for each planet. They're spot on.

'Could all entrants please take their places by their projects,' Ms Bayliss says.

'Good luck, *paidi mou*,' Yiayia whispers as Chloe kisses her and leaves us to stand by her diorama.

I scan the other entrants. There's twelve kids altogether with some impressive projects.

'I think that papier-mache volcano might be Chloe's biggest threat,' I say. 'What do you think, guys?'

'Quiet, girls,' Yiayia says. 'The judging is about to start.'

Ms Bayliss turns on a microphone. 'I'd like

to thank everyone for entering this year's fair,' she says. 'It's been tough to choose the finalists, but I've managed to narrow it down to four.'

I hold hands with Bella and Grace.

'The finalists are: Jeremy Kleban, Joshua Gardner, Liam Campbell...'

I gasp. I think my heart skips a beat too.

'...and Chloe Karalis!'

Bella and Grace squeal.

I exhale in relief.

The unsuccessful entrants join the crowd while everyone sizes up the finalists.

Jeremy has made a cardboard maze for a mouse, Liam's grown a tomato seedling and Joshua built the papier-mache volcano.

'That volcano does look good,' Grace says. 'Joshua will give Chloe a run for her money.'

Ms Bayliss taps the microphone to get our attention. 'All four finalists did a wonderful job, but there can only be one winner.'

I cross my fingers and toes for Chloe.

'There was one particular project that stood out,' Ms Bayliss says. 'And I think you'll all see why in a moment. Lights, please.'

We're suddenly standing in darkness.

'What's going on?' I ask.

Yiayia chuckles. 'You'll soon see,' she says. 'My Chloe has a surprise for you.'

Everyone cranes their necks to look up in awe. *Ooooooooooh. Aaaaaaaaaah.*

Images of the actual planets and hundreds of stars glow from the ceiling.

'Where is it coming from?' Bella asks.

'Chloe, of course,' I say.

I should've known she'd have more than fruit up her sleeve.

The lights flick back on. Ms Bayliss pulls a blue sticker from her coat pocket.

'Those images came from a homemade slide projector behind Chloe Karalis's diorama,' she says. 'So, not only has Chloe introduced us to the world of astronomy through her diorama of the solar system, she has also used principles of physics by assembling a device that projects light onto a distant surface. I think we can all agree that her extra effort is deserving of first place.'

Grace, Bella and I leap into the air and cheer with all our might.

Yiayia lets out a hoot and does a little dance, which makes us all laugh.

Chloe waves as Ms Bayliss slaps the blue sticker on Jupiter.

Mission Lab Coat: complete.

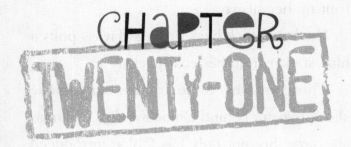

CHAPTER TWENTY-ONE

I wake up with a start.

'Ava, it's six in the morning! What do you want?' I hiss.

Ava is standing over me with her face so close to mine, I can feel her breath on my cheek. She looks as if she's about to burst into tears. I didn't mean to sound so harsh. I'm just sleepy, and Mum made me go to bed in hair rollers which have been digging into my scalp for about ten hours now.

'I don't want to go in the pageant,' Ava says. 'I'm not pretty enough. I won't win.'

My sister's words make my heart ache. This is exactly the reason the Anti-Princess Club planned its fourth mission. No one should be judged on their prettiness. Especially five-year-olds like Ava.

I pull back my doona and Ava snuggles up beside me. I think carefully about what to say. It's too late for her to pull out of the pageant. Mum has already bought her dress and made all the arrangements.

'Ava, you are the prettiest girl I know,' I say. 'But it's all about maths. It depends on odds and averages.'

Ava doesn't understand. She's only just mastering addition and subtraction, which is impressive for a five-year-old. But I try again.

'The problem with these things is that it depends who the judges are on the day,' I say. 'The judges there today might think black hair is pretty, so because you have red hair, they might not give you a lot of points. Another judge on a different day might think red hair is prettier than black hair.'

Ava sighs. 'Well, can we find out what the judges like before it starts?'

'No, that's the problem,' I say. 'All you can do is smile and try to have fun. If you don't win, it's not your fault. If I was the judge, you'd win for sure.'

It's been a long night. I hosted a sleepover for the Anti-Princess Club so we could plot our final mission. Mum thinks the girls are here to support me in the beauty pageant – which they are, but not in the way she imagines.

The other anti-princesses stir in their sleeping bags. Bella's eyes are the first to open.

'Good morning, beauty queen,' she says. 'Erk, beauty queen sounds even more spew-worthy than princess.'

Mum is banging some pots and pans down in the kitchen. 'Wake up, girls,' she calls. 'It's pageant day!'

Chloe and Grace make spewing sounds from their sleeping bags.

'Let the final mission begin,' I say.

We get dressed and head downstairs to where breakfast is waiting for us.

'Now don't stuff yourself with food, Emily,' Mum says. 'You don't want a bulging tummy in your pageant dress.'

I ignore her and scoff three pieces of toast plus a banana. I also grab a yoghurt for the road.

Mum snatches the yoghurt from my hands and herds us outside to her van. We all squeeze in between the hanging frilly dresses, shoeboxes and a silver briefcase.

'Here we go,' I whisper. 'The final mission begins.'

The trip to the hall where the pageant is being held takes about half an hour. None of the anti-princesses says a word for the whole drive.

'You must be nervous, girls,' Mum says from the driver's seat.

'Yup,' I manage. It's not a lie. I *am* nervous. I'm scared of the mission not working out.

We pull up in a car park full of mums and daughters flapping around like noisy galahs. I wave goodbye to the anti-princesses at the main entrance as Mum puts her arms around Ava and me to direct us through the back door for contestants.

What we walk into is like another planet. It's a room lined with dressing tables and huge mirrors surrounded by light globes. There are

twice as many girls as chairs, and everyone is scrambling to find a space to get ready.

Mum grabs a chair and orders me to sit. I try to get up so Ava can take my place, but Mum gently pushes down on my shoulders so my butt can't move.

'Ava's not onstage until later, Emily,' she says. 'We need to concentrate on you right now.'

She snaps open the latches of her briefcase. There are pots of powder and glitter, tubes of lipstick and cream, and at least a dozen sponges and brushes of all different shapes and sizes.

I sigh with relief when Mum starts to unravel the rollers on my head. As she takes them out, the unrolled strands spring up into spirals around my face like hundreds of tiny slinkies.

'Don't you just love it?' Mum asks.

Ava pulls a face and pokes her fingers into her mouth. 'Mummy, why didn't you just leave Emily's hair the way it was? You always talk about how pretty it is, so why are you changing it?'

I love my sister. She's such an anti-princess in the making.

Mum ignores Ava and takes a sponge out of the briefcase. She dips it in brown gunk and starts rubbing it on my forehead.

'Yuck!' Ava shrieks. 'It looks like mud.'

Mum plonks down the soggy sponge. 'You're not helping here, Ava. I'm taking you to Emily's friends. They can look after you in the main hall.'

I freeze.

'Act cool, Emily,' I mutter to myself. 'You can't blow your cover now. The anti-princesses will figure out what to do with Ava.'

Mum comes back into the dressing room and picks up the sponge. Before long my whole face is two shades darker. Then my eyelids are painted purple, my lips pink and my cheeks orange. If I was a circus clown, this might make sense.

I can't take my eyes off myself in the mirror – partly because I look so strange and partly because I'm too embarrassed to turn around.

'My oh my, Emily, I could just eat you up!' It's Hungry behind me.

'You remember Fiona, don't you, Emily?' Mum asks. 'She'll be onstage with you today.'

I turn to face Hungry and wait for the rest of the girls in the room to point their fingers at me and start laughing. But they don't. 'All of you girls look so *pretty*!' Hungry shrieks.

I scan the room in disbelief. We all look the same. We all have gunk on our faces, big curly hair and glitter everywhere. Even our dresses are the same. There are different colours, but they're all sparkly, pouffy and extremely uncomfortable.

'Ten minutes, everyone,' Hungry calls. 'Finish off that make-up.'

Mum looks edgy, but I feel a hundred times worse. Maybe a thousand times worse. No, at least a hundred thousand times worse.

'Do you want me to come with you, Emily?' Mum asks.

'No,' I say quickly. 'You better go and get Ava. My friends will want to watch me when I'm onstage. They won't be able to look after a five-year-old at the same time.'

Mum falls for it. *Phew.*

I suddenly feel an extra pang of guilt.

'I love you, Mum,' I say. 'I hope you'll be proud of me.'

Mum gives me a light hug so as not to squash my dress and an air kiss to avoid smudging my make-up. 'Of course I'll be proud of you, Emily.'

I make my way to the wings with the other contestants. The smell of hairspray makes me want to sneeze.

I take my place behind twelve girls, all waiting for their turn to go onstage. Broadway-style, cheesy music starts to play over the loudspeaker before a voice drowns it out.

It's Hungry.

CHAPTER TWENTY-TWO

'What's your favourite place to go shopping, Pollyanna?' Hungry asks.

What boring questions. I wonder what she'll ask me when it's my turn onstage.

'Psssst, Emily,' Bella whispers from behind a curtain. 'Are you ready?'

The girl in front of me turns around. 'What was that? Is there someone there?'

We can't get caught out. Not now when we're so close to the stage.

'It's just my mum,' I say. 'She needs to fix something on my dress.'

I slip behind the curtain where the anti-princesses are armed and ready.

'Quickly,' I whisper. 'There's only a minute or two at the most before it's my turn.'

Bella rubs my face with a washcloth and pulls my hair into a ponytail. Chloe unzips my dress and slips a T-shirt over my head. Grace helps me step into some tracksuit pants and sneakers.

'And now, let's welcome to the stage... *Emily!*' Hungry booms over the microphone.

'You're ready,' Chloe says. 'Go now!'

I step out from behind the curtain and zoom onto the stage before anyone has a chance to stop me. The music comes to an abrupt halt.

I hear gasps and murmurs from the crowd, but I can't make out what anyone's saying. I force a smile at Hungry, whose mouth is gaping.

'I'm ready for my question,' I say.

Hungry shuffles some cards in her hands and clears her throat. She looks horrified.

'Um, well…ahem,' she says. 'Okay, Emily. What is your favourite fairytale?'

I take the microphone from her hand and walk to the front of the stage. The lights are so bright that I can't make out anyone's faces. It's probably a good thing that I can't see Mum.

I clear my throat and begin.

'I don't have a favourite fairytale. And that's because fairytales aren't very fair at all. My friends and I call them *unfair*ytales.'

Hungry calls from behind me, 'Okay, Emily, you can leave the stage now.'

'I'm not finished,' I say into the microphone. 'I need to explain why fairytales are unfair. They are unfair because the girls in fairytales are never the heroes. They're almost always princesses who need rescuing by princes. That's why my friends and I decided to form the Anti-Princess Club. We don't want to be treated like princesses. WE. DON'T. NEED. RESCUING.'

'That's very nice, Emily,' Hungry calls again. 'It's time to leave the stage now, thank you.'

'One more thing,' I say. 'You know what else is unfair? Beauty pageants. Girls shouldn't be judged on their prettiness. We're *all* pretty, and we don't need to slop gunk on our faces or wear silly dresses to prove it.'

Hungry clears her throat and jabs her finger towards the wings.

'And you know what else?' I ask. 'There are so many things that are *way* more interesting than being pretty. I bet there are all sorts of awesome girls in this room – awesome writers, trumpet players, high jumpers, skateboarders, even scuba divers. I know there is at least one awesome scientist, athlete and designer here.'

The stage lights dim. Hungry is trying everything to get me out of the spotlight now.

'Keep going!' calls a familiar voice from the back of the hall.

It can't be. I shade my eyes with my hand and squint over the audience. It *is*. It's my dad.

'I, I…' my voice quivers. 'I want my mum and dad to know I love them. I'm not doing this to make you angry, Mum. I'm doing it to show girls that they don't have to be princesses if they don't want to.'

I put the microphone on the floor and rush

offstage past Hungry and her furious face. I think I might have seen actual steam shooting out of her ears.

There's a clap. Then another. *Clap, clap. Clap. Clap.* It turns into applause. It turns into cheering. It turns into chanting.

'*No more princesses! No more princesses!*' the crowd yells.

I see the anti-princesses on the other side of the stage. They're holding hands, jumping up and down and squealing. Bella gives me a thumbs-up.

Mission Tiara: complete.

EPILOGUE

Ava refused to go onstage after me, but luckily Mum was so happy to see Dad that it took the focus off us. He wanted to surprise us when he got home from his latest Army stint two days early.

Dad is still very impressed by my speech. He says the look on Hungry's face was hilarious, as if she didn't know whether to snatch the microphone from me or let me speak.

Even Mum admitted the whole pageant thing was a bit too stressful for her liking. All that build-up and competition gave her heart palpitations. She says I convinced her that kids shouldn't be judged on their looks – even though she still insists Ava and I are the prettiest girls in the world. She also says she's going to stick to beautifying grown women from now on.

Of course, I didn't win the pageant. It would have been very weird if a girl in tracksuit pants walked out with a tiara on her head.

I did win a different sort of crown, though. The anti-princesses decided to make me the leader of the club. They figured every organisation has a president or a captain, and I guess they chose me because I called that first meeting that got it all started.

It's not just the four of us to organise now. It seems my speech inspired a few of the girls in the audience. Well, more than a few. The mathematical term would be one hundred and two. That's right. The Anti-Princess Club has one hundred and two members plus Bella, Grace, Chloe and me – that's one hundred and six altogether.

About half of those members are girls who approached me at the pageant. But then my inbox got swamped after a video of my speech went viral online. There are loads of new anti-princesses that I've signed up but haven't even met in real life.

Our treehouse isn't big enough for everyone, so I came up with a new idea. I built a website that's now an online club where members can chat to each other. Bella designed a banner and did a few illustrations for the homepage.

Sometimes I help the younger members with maths homework in our chatroom, and Chloe jumps online if anyone needs help with science. Offline, a few of the anti-princesses from our school formed an Anti-Princess Club soccer team with Grace as their coach.

The original club members still hold an official meeting at least once a week. We alternate between the treehouse and Chloe's apartment because we love hanging out with Yiayia.

Baklava, HQ, Lab Coat and Tiara were our first missions, but they won't be our last. I can't wait to see what crazy codenames will land in my notepad next. I wish I could come up with a formula or equation to figure out what our future missions will be.

Whatever lies ahead, there's one thing I'm certain of: we won't need rescuing.